THE Princess IN BLACK
and the PRINCE IN PINK

THE *Princess* IN
BLACK
and the PRINCE IN PINK

Shannon Hale & Dean Hale

illustrated by
LeUyen Pham

CANDLEWICK PRESS

Text copyright © 2023 by Shannon and Dean Hale
Illustrations copyright © 2023 by LeUyen Pham

First edition 2023

Library of Congress Catalog Card Number 2022936840
ISBN 978-1-5362-0978-5

23 24 25 26 27 28 LEO 10 9 8 7 6 5 4 3 2 1

Printed in Heshan, Guangdong, China

This book was typeset in LTC Kennerley Pro.
The illustrations were done in watercolor and ink.

Candlewick Press
99 Dover Street
Somerville, Massachusetts 02144

www.candlewick.com

For Milo and Felix,
who save the day in their own unique ways
SH and DH

To Sam, the Prince of All Colors
of the Rainbow
LP

Chapter 1

Princess Magnolia and Frimplepants set out when the sun was still low and shy. It wasn't far to Princess Snapdragon's castle. But they did not want to be late for the Flower Festival. It was the biggest event of the season!

During the day, there was a fair. And in the evening, a ball. Princess Snapdragon had asked Princess Magnolia to be in charge of the ball. It was a big responsibility.

When she arrived, the Flower Festival Fair was already in full swing. And full of people! Clearly nobody had wanted to be late.

Princess Orchid waved to her from the Rosemary-Go-Round. Princesses Apple Blossom and Honeysuckle were helping kids in the Bumper Bees. Princesses Hyacinth and Bluebell drove the Solar Coaster. And Princess Posy worked at the Lily Pond.

"Hello, Princess Magnolia!" said Princess Snapdragon. She eyed the overflowing cart Frimplepants was pulling. "Do you need help unloading?"

"Yes, thank you," said Princess Magnolia. "I brought so many things for the ball."

"Oh, how I hope it is a success!" said Princess Snapdragon. "I think the ball is the most important part of the Flower Festival. The ball and the fennel cakes."

Princess Sneezewort was neck-deep in fennel cakes. She waved.

Princess Magnolia yearned to make the ball a success. So she came prepared. *Very* prepared.

Princess Snapdragon lifted a box out of the cart. "Wow, what is in all of these?"

"Decorations!" said Princess Magnolia. "This one is food decorations. This one is door decorations. This one is wall decorations. And this one . . . is a special, secret decoration."

"A special, secret decoration?" Princess Snapdragon leaned closer. "You can tell me."

And Princess Magnolia was about to tell. But just then, somebody screamed.

Chapter 2

A scream? Was someone in trouble?
"Oh no," said Princess Snapdragon.
"Maybe a monster is attacking the
Flower Festival!"

That would not be good. Princess Magnolia was prepared to decorate the ball. She was not prepared to fight a monster. For that, she'd need to change into the Princess in Black. But she was worried. If she went to change, she'd have to leave her decorations.

And then she saw the cause of the trouble. It was not a monster. It was a bird. A big, flightless bird.

"EMU!" shrieked a tiny girl.

The emu stomped straight through the crowd. Kids had to scramble out of the way. A garbage can blocked its path. Did the emu go around the garbage can? No, it did not. It kicked the can. Hard.

The crowd gasped. This wasn't just a big bird. This was a grumpy bird. The grumpiest bird anyone had ever seen.

The emu looked from side to side, as if daring anyone to stop it.

"Stop it!" said Princess Magnolia. She didn't know what else to do. If it were a monster, she would wage battle. But what should she do with an emu?

The emu walked up to her. Its legs were like two tree trunks. It stared straight at her with menacing eyes. And then, it kicked one of her boxes.

The crowd gasped again.

"That's not nice," said Princess Magnolia. "You can't just kick people's things."

The emu looked from side to side in an alarming way. Then it lifted its heavy foot and stomped. Right on the special, secret box. The box crumpled with a sound of breaking glass.

Princess Magnolia stared at the broken pieces of her special, secret decoration. How could the ball be a success now?

Chapter 3

Back, beast!"

Who said that? Not the Princess in Black. Princess Magnolia had been too confused by the emu to change into the Princess in Black.

No, it was a knight. A knight in shining armor.

The emu tried to kick the knight. Its foot dented the armor. But the knight still stood.

"A fair is no place for a kicking emu," said the knight. He held his lance sideways with both hands. And like a snowplow, he moved forward.

The emu walked backward. Back-
ward all the way through the fair.
Under the Solar Coaster. Past the
Spring Toss game. And out the gate.
Princess Snapdragon closed it shut.

The crowd cheered!

Princess Magnolia didn't feel like cheering. She was staring at the crushed boxes. She thought she had been prepared for everything. But she had not been prepared for a grumpy emu.

The knight bowed to her. "I am Prince Valerian. And you look sad. Can I help you?"

"I don't think so," she said. "You helped with the emu. But I don't need a knight's help. What I really need is a hero that fixes decorations and ruined balls."

"Yes!" said Prince Valerian.

"What?" said Princess Magnolia.

"Uh . . . I mean . . . alas!" said Prince Valerian. "Alas that I'm only a knight! And not a party hero. So. I should go now. I need to go . . . grocery shopping . . . for my fish. My fish needs groceries . . ."

He ran off.

"Alas," said Princess Magnolia. "Alas, alas." It felt like a good word to say when she was feeling sad and hopeless.

She wanted to ask for help. But her friends were busy with their own responsibilities. And Princess Snapdragon was fixing other messes. The emu had kicked a lot of stuff.

Princess Magnolia and Frimple-pants dragged her crushed boxes into the castle. A ball was a big responsibility. And just then, it felt too big, even for a princess and a unicorn.

Chapter 4

Prince Valerian ducked into the empty Fun with Fertilizer tent. All his life, he had yearned for a chance to show his special skills. And at last, the day had come!

FUN WITH FERTILIZER

He put on each well-considered piece of his costume.

Tall, shiny boots with good soles for dancing.

Tasseled gloves to make each move-ment a show.

Sparkly mask
to add mystery.

And a tiara
for confidence.

He was no longer Prince Valerian.

He sneaked out of the tent.
Past the fair. Into the castle.
And entered the empty ball-
room in a storm of sparkles.

"Flourish!" he declared.

Princess Magnolia was alone, sitting on the ballroom floor and going through her crushed boxes. She seemed surprised to see him. Or perhaps . . . delighted?

"Who are you?" she asked with surprise. Or delight.

"I am the Prince in Pink!" said the Prince in Pink. "Champion of celebrations! Paladin of parties! Darling of discos! Wherever there is a festival in distress, there I will be with a helping hand." He shook a tasseled glove.

"Alas, I don't think anyone can help," said Princess Magnolia. She showed him the special, secret decoration. It looked like a box full of broken mirrors. "It was a disco ball. I was going to hang it in the ballroom. The lights would have sparkled on its many mirrored surfaces.

And the sparkles would make people feel like dancing. But now it's ruined. And there's no way to fix it."

Aha! Forget monsters and grumpy emus. This was the kind of challenge that the Prince in Pink liked.

He pulled ribbons from his belt and scissors from his holster. He cut some ribbon, attached it to a piece of broken mirror, and lifted up his sparkly creation. "Flourish!"

"Oh! That's a great idea!" said Princess Magnolia. Definitely with delight.

And so Princess Magnolia and the Prince in Pink waged decorations.

BOUQUET BOUNCE!✿

CUP-CAKE CRAM!✿

Chapter 5

Emu stalked away from the festival. She kicked the dirt with her powerful legs. Her legs were made for two things: kicking and dancing. And she was good at both. Very, very good.

It wasn't fair. She wanted to party. She yearned to dance. But nobody thought about Emu. Nobody invited *her* to balls.

Well, she was going anyway. She would grab her girlfriends the Ostrich Twins. Together they were a gang. The Flightless Bird Herd. Everybody knew not to mess with the Flightless Bird Herd.

Well, everybody who was a bird.

But the featherless ones would learn too.

The Flightless Bird Herd wouldn't just go to that ball. They would CRASH that ball. And if those featherless twerps didn't let them dance, they'd use their legs for the other thing.

Kicking. The other thing was kicking.

Chapter 6

The Flower Festival Ball was in full swing. The musicians played a funky tune. The lights glittered on all the disco ball pieces. And everyone was dancing.

"You did such a beautiful job," said Princess Snapdragon.

"I had help," said Princess Magnolia. "From the Prince in Pink."

"Who?" asked Princess Snapdragon.

Princess Magnolia looked around. Princess Sneezewort and Duff were doing the turkey trot. Princesses Orchid, Bluebell, and Posy were doing the bunny hop. And Prince Valerian was doing the twist. But the Prince in Pink was nowhere to be seen.

"That's funny," said Princess Magnolia. "I don't know where he went. And I never got a chance to thank him."

She walked around the ball to check on things. The decorations. The music. The snacks. It all seemed to be a big success!

She filled up the punch bowl. Then she noticed ripples on the surface of the punch. Ripples made by some loud, distant sound. Perhaps the stomping feet of the dancers? Or perhaps . . .

There was a heavy knock at the ballroom door.

The doors burst open. There stood
Emu, looking from side to side in an
alarming way. And beside her, two
enormous, menacing ostriches. They
opened their beaks and hissed.

Chapter 7

This time, Princess Magnolia was ready. She crawled under the snack table. When she slid out the other side, she was no longer Princess Magnolia. She was the Princess in Black!

"You may not ruin the ball!" said the Princess in Black.

"That's right!" said a bunch of other heroes.

The Princess in Black looked around. To her surprise—and delight—she saw the ballroom was now full of her hero friends. Her princess friends had mysteriously disappeared. And there! The Prince in Pink had returned!

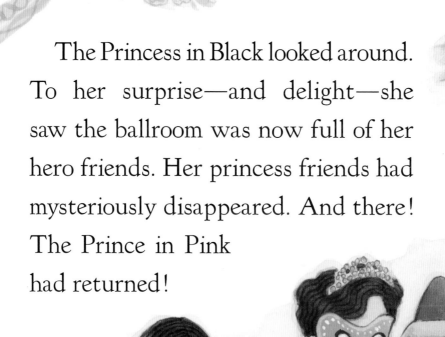

Emu stalked toward the musicians, her head bobbing on her long neck. *One-two.* The Ostrich Twins followed, their heavy feet clicking on the ballroom floor. *Three-four.* They all flapped their wings. *Five-six-seven-eight!*

The musicians started to tremble. The music stopped, and the ballroom went silent. Emu hissed. She stomped her three-toed foot.

"What do they want?" wondered the Prince in Pink.

"Hmm, I have an idea," said the Princess in Black. "Do you have your decorating tools?"

The Prince in Pink nodded. "I like the way you think."

And together, they waged make-over.

TWINKLE TWINKLE

GLITTER FLOURISH!

When the glitter cleared, the heroes in the ballroom gasped.

The grumpy birds were now fancy birds. The fanciest birds anyone had ever seen. Though still grumpy. Fancy, grumpy, flightless birds who were ready for some kicking.

Or maybe—just maybe—ready for that *other* thing.

Chapter 8

The Prince in Pink pulled a hand mirror from his holster. He showed the birds their reflection.

"Flourish!" he declared.

The Ostrich Twins preened. Emu's frowny beak slowly turned up. But then, she grunted. She growled. And she stuck out one big, powerful leg.

Was she still in a kicking mood? The heroes struck battle poses.

But if the Princess in Black had guessed right, they didn't need battle poses.

She took a careful step toward Emu. Emu took a careful step back.

Emu took a big step forward. The Princess in Black took a big step back.

"That's the idea," said the Prince in Pink.

He joined her. Heroes stepped forward, birds stepped back. Birds forward, heroes back.

"Wait . . ." said Miss Fix-It. "They're . . . they're dancing?"

"I think so," said the Princess in Black. "All we need is—"

"Music!" shouted Flower Girl.

The musicians lifted their instruments.
And then, everyone waged dance party.

FLIGHTLESS FOXTROT!

FEATHERY WHIRL!

TWINKLE TWINKLE

TOTAL TWIRL!

Chapter 9

It was late. The Princess in Black had rosy cheeks from dancing. And a tired tummy from laughing. The ball had been a big success. She looked for the Prince in Pink, eager to thank him. She spotted him sneaking out the ballroom door.

"Are you leaving?" she asked, following him into the quiet night.

The Prince in Pink nodded. "My work here . . . is done."

"You were a big help," she said. "And if your kingdom ever needs help with monsters, you can call on me."

"I will let my friend Prince Valerian know," said the Prince in Pink. "He's usually the one who handles monsters."

The Princess in Black looked around. "Where is Prince Valerian? I should thank him too."

The Prince in Pink unraveled a ribbon from his belt. He threw one end to lasso the top of the Solar Coaster.

"I'm sure Prince Valerian will be back soon," he said. "But if you ever need a party hero, the Prince in Pink is at your service!"

He threw down a glitter bomb.

When the glitter cleared,
the Prince in Pink was gone.

The Princess in Black smiled. "I'll be sure to let Princess Magnolia know. She's the one who handles parties."